Who Wants a DRAGON?

For Gabriel the Bold!
With love from your dad

For Molly the Menace!
With love from your fairy godmother, Lindsey

First published in Great Britain in 2004 by Orchard Books London.

ISBN 0-439-80079-X

12 11 10 9 8 7 6 5 4 3 2 1   5 6 7 8 9 10/0

Printed in the U.S.A.   08

This edition first printing, September 2005

Who Wants a DRAGON?

By James Mayhew ✳ **Illustrated by Lindsey Gardiner**

SCHOLASTIC INC.
New York Toronto London Auckland Sydney
Mexico City New Delhi Hong Kong Buenos Aires

Who wants a dragon?

All fiery and bright?

A lost baby dragon,
alone in the night?

Who wants a dragon?

This witch in a hat?

A dragon is much more
fun than a cat!

But dragons are not the best thing for a broom.

They're bigger than cats
and there's not enough room!

Who wants a dragon?

This knight brave and bold?

How could he leave him outside in the cold?

But inside his helmet
the knight's in a fright.
He's certain the dragon
will give him a bite!

Who wants a dragon?

This sleepy princess?

Look out, though, he's got muddy
paws on her dress!

Poor little dragon, all in a muddle.

There must be someone who'll give you a cuddle!

Who wants a dragon?

This King or his Queen?

Nobody wants him,
not even this fairy.

Everyone seems to
think he's too scary.

There must be someone,
somewhere out there,

who'd cuddle a
dragon with love
to spare.

**Poor little dragon
alone in the night.**

**But look! Here comes someone
who'll love him just right.**

She'll cuddle him, and kiss him,

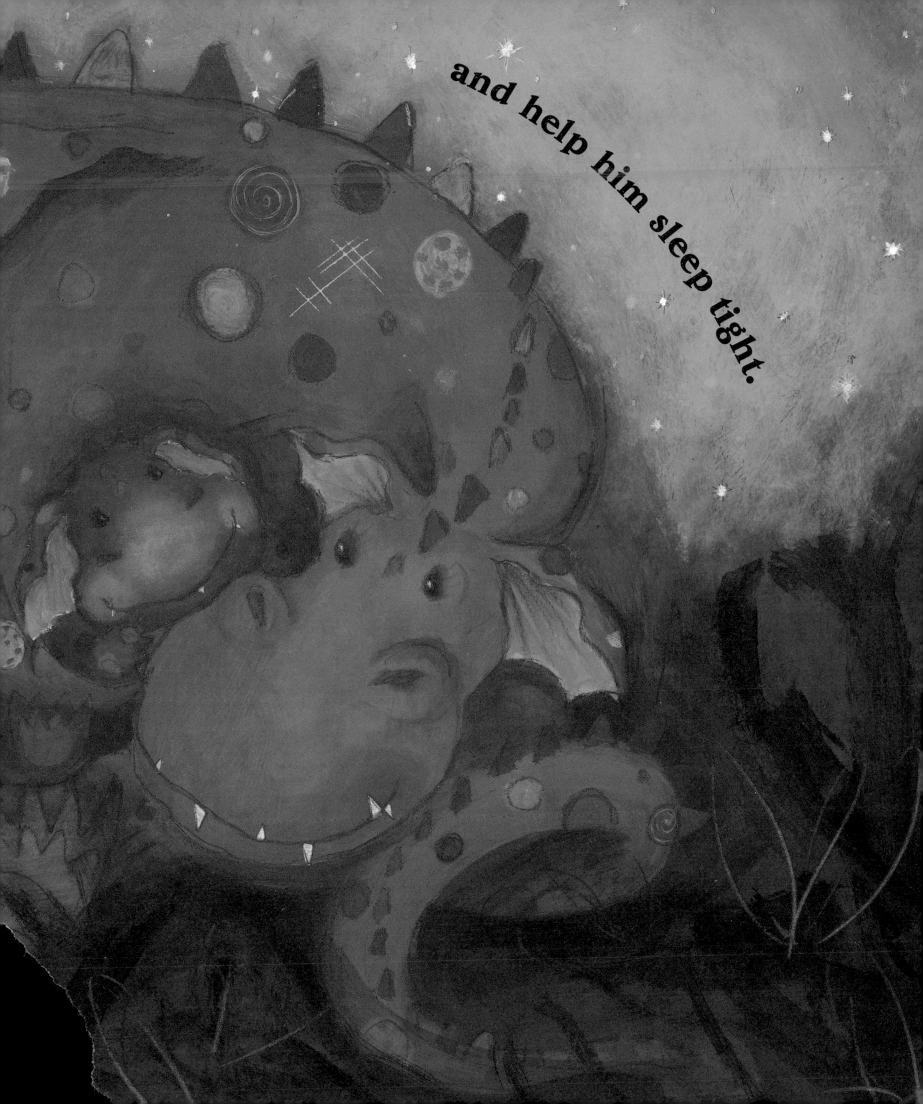

and help him sleep tight.